W9-CNA-466

Hide and Seek

Based on the teleplay by Susan Kim
Adapted by Laura F. Marsh

NATIONAL GEOGRAPHIC
WASHINGTON, D.C.

For Mason with love
— L.F.M.

Book design by Bea Jackson

Photo credits
pp 13 (tiger): zschnepf/ Shutterstock; pp 14 (green frog): Snowleopard1/ Shutterstock; pp 15 (blue frog): John Arnold/ Shutterstock; pp 18 (ptarmigan): Mark Yarchoan/ Shutterstock; pp 19 (chameleon): Mitja Mladkovic/ iStockPhoto; pp 20 (walking stick): Joel Sartore/National Geographic/Getty Images

 Founded in 1888, the National Geographic Society is one of the largest nonprofit scientific and educational organizations in the world. It reaches more than 285 million people worldwide each month through its official journal, NATIONAL GEOGRAPHIC, and its four other magazines; the National Geographic Channel; television documentaries; radio programs; films; books; videos and DVDs; maps; and interactive media. National Geographic has funded more than 8,000 scientific research projects and supports an education program combating geographic illiteracy.

For more information, please call
1-800-NGS LINE (647-5463) or write to the following address:
NATIONAL GEOGRAPHIC SOCIETY
1145 17th Street N.W., Washington, D.C. 20036-4688 U.S.A.

Visit us online at www.nationalgeographic.com/books
Librarians and teachers, visit us at www.ngchildrensbooks.org

For information about special discounts for bulk purchases, please contact National Geographic Books Special Sales: ngspecsales@ngs.org.

For rights or permissions inquiries, please contact National Geographic Books Subsidiary Rights: ngbookrights@ngs.org.

Library of Congress Cataloging-in-Publication Data available from the publisher on request.
Trade Paperback ISBN 978-1-4263-0305-0
Reinforced Library Edition ISBN 978-1-4263-0306-7

Printed in the United States of America

Everyone was playing hide and seek on the savanna.
"Ready or not, here I come!" called Max the elephant.

"I'm sorry, Karla," he said to his zebra friend. "I found you."

"Not again!" she sighed. "That's ten times in a row."

They decided to play again.
    As Bo the cheetah counted, Karla looked for a good place to hide.

But her friends could see her a mile away.

"Why don't you try curling up like this?" asked Bo.

"Or hiding next to a rock?" offered Max the elephant.

The monkeys showed how they hid in the tree branches.

"Guys, I can't climb trees or curl up into a ball. And if I stand in front of a rock, I'll look like a zebra standing in front of a rock!" Karla said. "What's the fun of hide and seek when you can't even hide?"

Later that day, Mama Mirabelle found Karla by the watering hole.

"What are you upset about, my little stripey friend?" Mama asked.

"It's my stripes that I'm upset about," she answered. "Why can't I just be all yellow or all gray? I stick out like a sore hoof!"

"Now, now Karla, lots of animals stick out.
That's what makes them so special!" Mama said. "I think I have
some movies that just might cheer you up."

"It's **Movie** Time!"

Mama showed everyone her friend, Raj the tiger.
"He's got as many stripes as you do, Karla – and
they're bright orange!"

"And these poison dart frogs have lots of bright colors and patterns," said Mama.

"Their colors scare away their enemies."

"But I just want to win at hide and seek once in a while!" Karla said.

Mama pulled out a great movie about hiding — about camouflage.
"Camouflage is when animals blend into the background because of how they look," explained Bo.
Mama told the animals that camouflage was one of the best ways to hide.

"Try to find the ptarmigan," said Mama,

"or the chameleon,"

"or even the walking stick insect. It's not as easy breezy as you might think."
The animals tried their hardest. It **wasn't** easy.

"Well, I can't change color, and I'm not shaped like a stick, but maybe I can use camouflage to hide," said Karla brightly.

"I bet you can!" Mama replied.

As Bo started counting again, all of the animals ran to hide.

"Ready or not, here I come!" shouted Bo. He looked all over. "Where'd she go?"

"Did Karla go home?" Max asked.

"Karla, where are you?" hollered Bo. "Come out, come out, wherever you are!"

With a giggle, Karla jumped out of the grass.

"Well, I think Karla is the new hide and seek champion!" Mama announced.

Everyone cheered.

"I can't wait until tomorrow," Karla said. "So we can play hide and seek again!"

But Bo was not so sure. "How about tag?" he asked with a grin.